MAYA'S CHILDREN

The Story of La Llorona

RUDOLFO ANAYA

ILLUSTRATED BY MARIA BACA

HYPERION BOOKS FOR CHILDREN
New York

To the children of New Mexico and the world, with love
—R. A.

To the children of Eugene Field Elementary School
—M. B.

Printed in Hong Kong by South China Printing Company (1988) Ltd.

First Edition
1 3 5 7 9 10 8 6 4 2

The artwork for each picture is prepared using gouache.

Book design and border illustrations by Stephanie Bart-Horvath.
This book is set in 15-point Hadriano.

Library of Congress Cataloging-in-Publication Data
Anaya, Rudolfo A.
Maya's Children /Rudolfo Anaya ; illustrated by Maria Baca. —1st ed.
p.   cm.
Summary: In ancient Mexico, the beautiful and magical grandchildren of the Sun
God are endangered by the threat of Señor Tiempo who, jealous of their
immortality, plots to destroy them.
ISBN 0-7868-0152-2 (trade)—ISBN 0-7868-2124-8 (lib. bdg.)
[1. Immortality—Fiction. 2. Mexico—Fiction.] I. Baca, Maria, ill. II. Title.
PZ7.A5186May 1996
[Fic]—dc20
95-41973

Author's Note

La Llorona, the crying woman, is a legendary creature who haunts rivers, lakes, and lonely roads. It is said she comes out at night, searching for her children. Her story is known throughout Latin America, where parents warn their own children to hurry home or La Llorona might grab them. As a child I heard many stories about her.

I wished to tell the story of La Llorona to very young readers without having her actually take the life of her children, as she does in the original story. In my retelling, La Llorona does not harm her children. Señor Tiempo becomes the bad guy, so to speak, and Maya *loses* her children to Time. Instead of using La Llorona as a character to frighten children—as she has been used by generations of parents—this story teaches youngsters about mortality. Through such motifs, I believe all myths or folktales can be adapted, especially for specific age-groups, to tell an interesting and valuable story.

I wish to thank the Rockefeller Foundation for a residency at the Bellagio Study Center in Italy, where the first draft of this story was written. Looking from the promontory across the incredible beauty of Lake Como and walking on the trails of that primeval forest, I once again heard La Llorona. Her anguished cry reminded me that I had heard her as a child when I played along the Pecos River in New Mexico. Her cry urged me to tell her story to children everywhere.

—Rudolfo Anaya

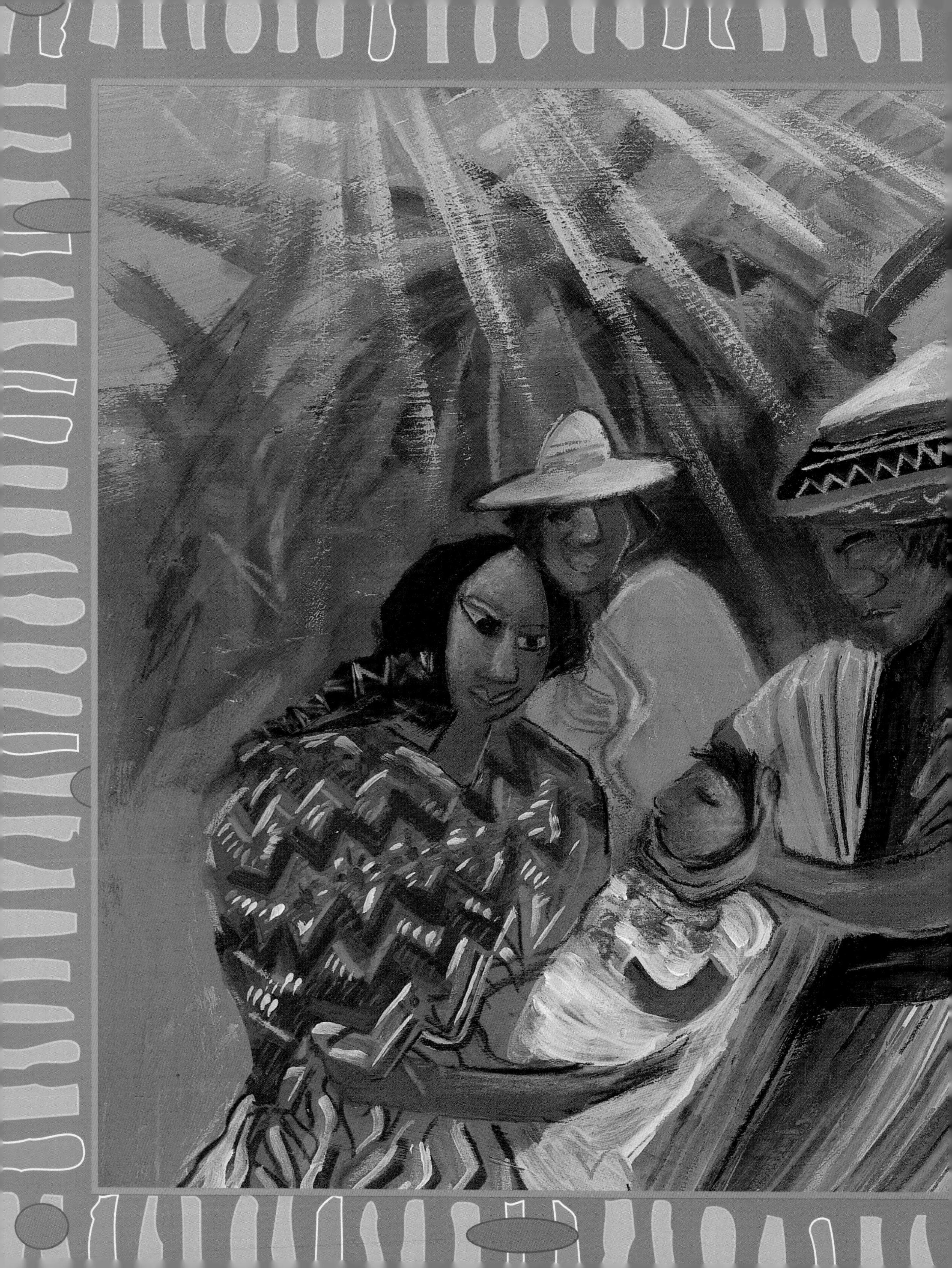

ong ago in ancient Mexico the villagers at the foot of a tall volcano celebrated the Festival of the Sun. On that day, too, a child was born. She was called Maya. When the chief priest was called to bless the child, he noticed a birthmark that looked like a shining sun on her shoulder.

Maya is a child of the Sun God, the chief priest thought. She is destined to be immortal. Not wanting to alarm the parents, he said nothing.

aya lived a happy life, helping her parents with their work in the fields and learning the ways of the village. She grew into a lovely young woman, adored by the villagers for her beauty and wisdom.

All the gods, too, admired Maya. All except Señor Tiempo, the god of time. He allotted each person their stay on earth. When he learned that Maya was destined to be immortal, he grew angry.

"This girl will live forever!" he cried. "I cannot change that, but I will find a way to ensure her children are not immortal!"

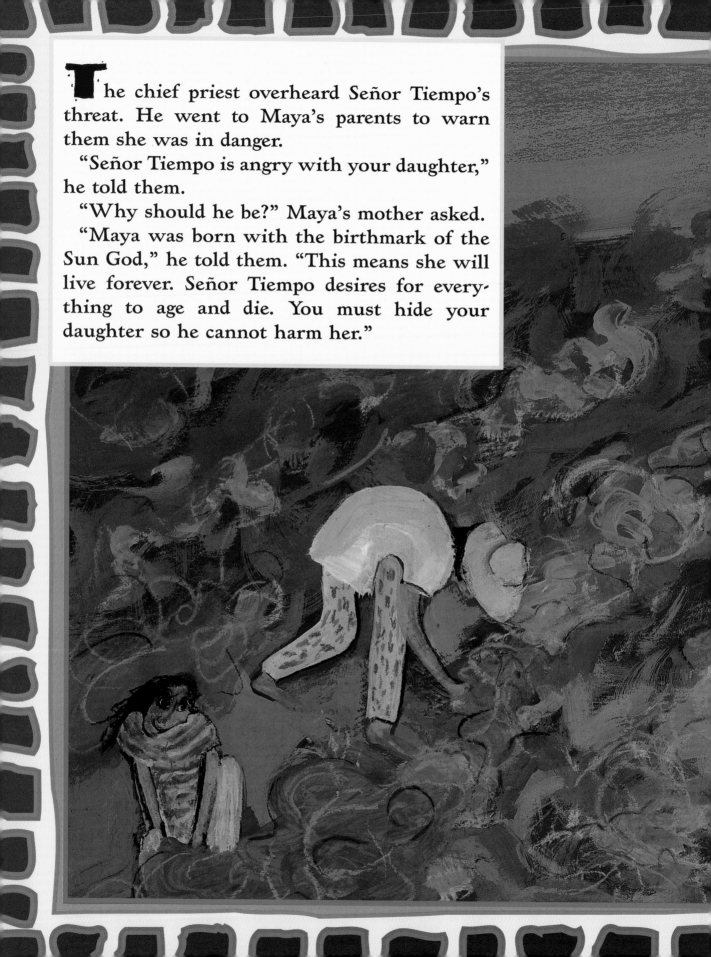

The chief priest overheard Señor Tiempo's threat. He went to Maya's parents to warn them she was in danger.

"Señor Tiempo is angry with your daughter," he told them.

"Why should he be?" Maya's mother asked.

"Maya was born with the birthmark of the Sun God," he told them. "This means she will live forever. Señor Tiempo desires for everything to age and die. You must hide your daughter so he cannot harm her."

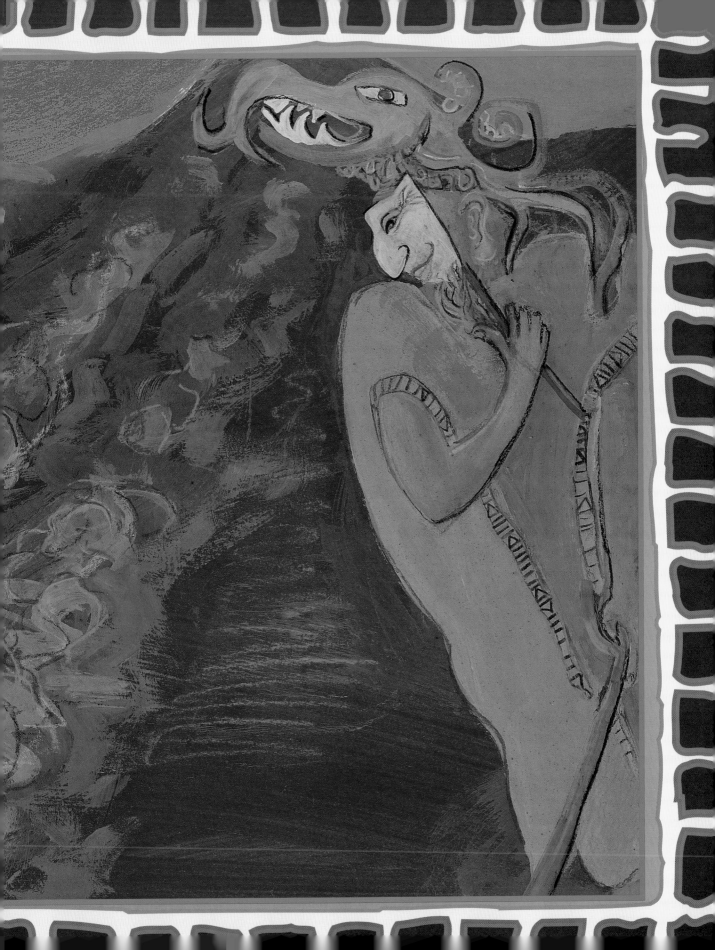

aya's parents feared for their daughter, so they took her up the mountain into the jungle. There, at the edge of a clear lake, Maya would live alone, away from the angry Señor Tiempo.

In the mornings Maya tended her vegetable garden. In the afternoons she went into the jungle to gather the bright feathers that fell from the wings of parrots. Gold, green, red, and blue feathers—these she wove into beautiful baskets.

As time passed, Maya became lonely and yearned for companionship.

"I am alone," she told the owl of the forest. "I wish some-one could come to live with me."

"It is time for you to have children," the owl replied.

These words made Maya happy. Children would be wonderful companions. She would watch over them and care for them.

"What must I do?" she asked the owl.

"**M**ake a clay bowl when the new moon appears in the night sky. When the moon is full, you must fill the pot with the fertile soil by the lake. Then you will be given seeds to plant in the pot."

Maya did as she was told. When the moon was new, she took red clay and made a beautiful earthen bowl. It was large and round, and Maya painted brightly colored birds on it. Later in the month, when the moon was full, she went to the lake to fill the bowl with earth.

As Maya was scooping the dark earth into the bowl, a friendly young man who grew corn in the valley came walking by.

"That is a beautiful vessel," he said. "Why are you filling it with earth?"

"I am making a child so I will not be lonely," Maya replied.

"You must put seeds into the bowl," he said. "In this way you will grow a lovely child."

He sat beside her and took kernels of corn from the leather pouch he carried. With great care he planted the corn in the pot and added sweet water from the lake.

aya thanked the young man and returned home. She placed the vessel on her window ledge. Every night the moon shone on the clay bowl, and in the day the sun warmed it.

One night, many months later, when the moon was in the last quarter, Maya heard a whimper. In the bowl, curled up, was a baby girl. Maya was delighted. She took the baby, wrapped her in a cotton blanket, and held her close.

"You are as beautiful as the bright tassels of the corn plant," she said, "so I will call you Corn Maiden."

The animals of the jungle came to admire the new baby.

"Señor Tiempo resents Maya," the snake reminded those present. "He cannot have her, but he will come to claim her child."

Maya grew fearful. "What can I do?" she asked the owl.

"Save the bowl by your fireplace," the owl replied. "If you save the clay in which Corn Maiden was born, Señor Tiempo cannot harm her." Maya did as she was told.

The new moon came, and Maya decided to make a second child. She made another bowl, and when the moon was full, she went to the edge of the lake to fill the pot with earth.

Another young man came walking by, a handsome young man who grew chile in the valley. When he asked what she was doing, Maya told him. He sat by her and added chile seeds to the soil.

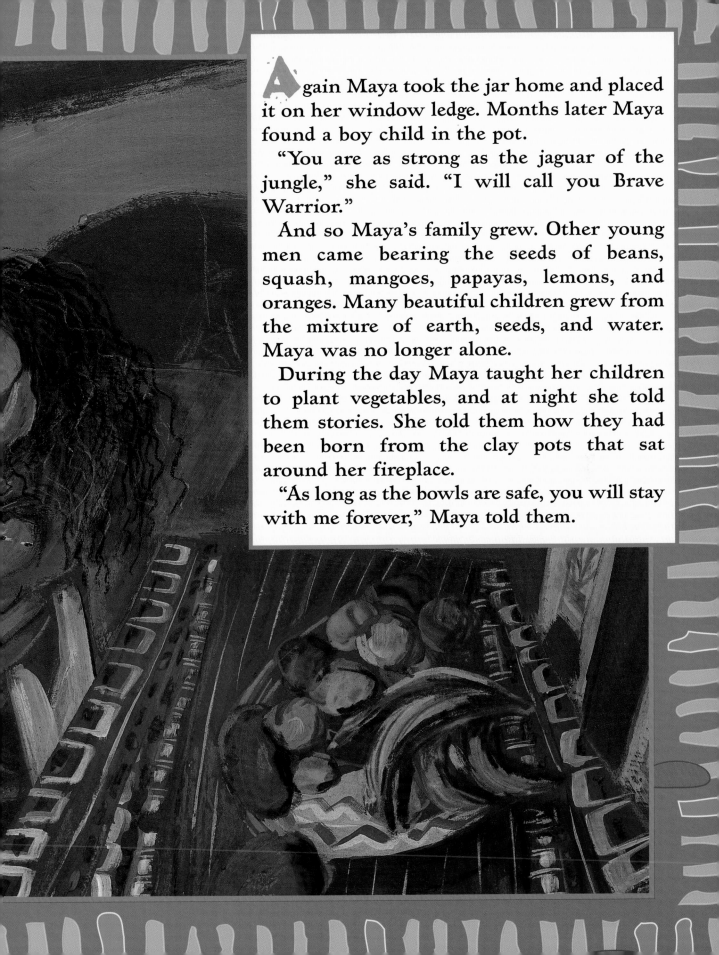

Again Maya took the jar home and placed it on her window ledge. Months later Maya found a boy child in the pot.

"You are as strong as the jaguar of the jungle," she said. "I will call you Brave Warrior."

And so Maya's family grew. Other young men came bearing the seeds of beans, squash, mangoes, papayas, lemons, and oranges. Many beautiful children grew from the mixture of earth, seeds, and water. Maya was no longer alone.

During the day Maya taught her children to plant vegetables, and at night she told them stories. She told them how they had been born from the clay pots that sat around her fireplace.

"As long as the bowls are safe, you will stay with me forever," Maya told them.

One night Señor Tiempo was lurking outside the home of Maya's parents. He overheard Maya's mother say, "Our daughter is safe in her home by the lake."

"Yes," Maya's father said. "Perhaps now she has escaped the vengeance of Señor Tiempo."

"Now I know where Maya is hiding," Señor Tiempo said. "I will pay her a visit."

Señor Tiempo disguised himself as a wise old teacher, one who travels the roads and gives good advice. He appeared at Maya's hut, where she and her children were harvesting corn.

"Where did you get these beautiful children?" Señor Tiempo asked Maya.

"I make bowls of clay and fill them with the earth by the lake," Maya answered. "Young men bring seeds of corn, squash, chile, and mangoes to plant in them. The seed pots are blessed by the moon and the sun, and so my children are born."

Señor Tiempo looked at her children. There were many daughters and many sons. Their skin glowed, their dark eyes were bright, and their long, black hair fell over their shoulders and glistened in the sun. All were happy and handsome.

Señor Tiempo grew angry. These beautiful children would live forever. He had to think of a way to steal Maya's children and make them his own.

oon your children will grow up and go away," Señor Tiempo said to Maya. "They will age and die."

"No," Maya answered. "The owl told me that as long as I keep the clay bowls of their birth, my children will also be immortal."

"But someone can steal those beautiful bowls," Señor Tiempo said. "I know how you can keep your children with you forever."

"I do not wish to lose my children," Maya said. "Tell me, what must I do?"

"Take the clay bowls in which your children were formed," Señor Tiempo said. "Break each pot and throw the pieces in the lake. That way your children will live forever."

Maya believed him and did as she was told. She broke all the clay bowls she had saved by her fireplace, went to the lake, and threw the clay pieces into the water.

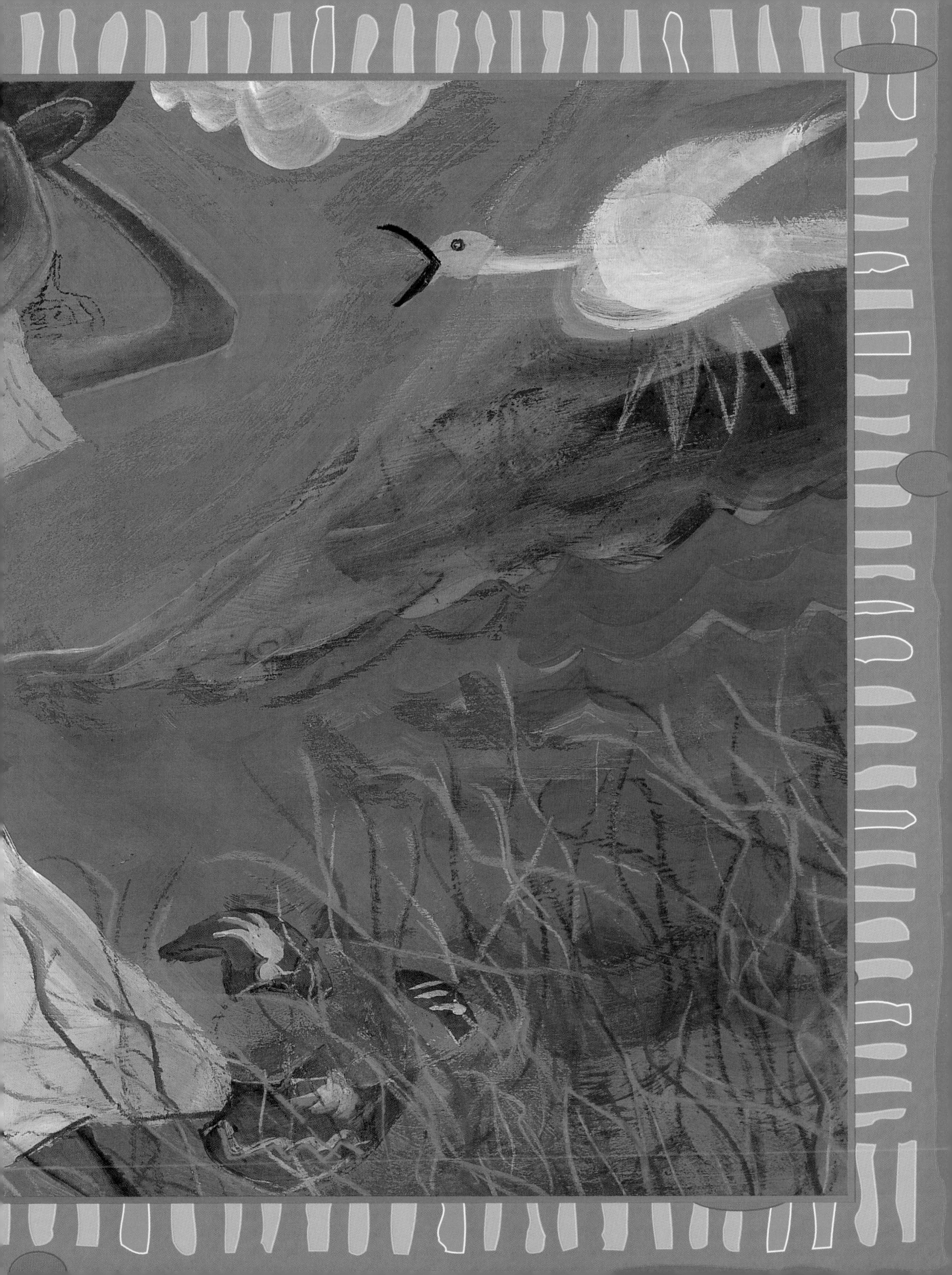

At that instant a terrible storm came over the lake. Lightning flashed, and thunder shook the jungle. The birds and animals hid in their nests and caves. Maya's children grew frightened.

"Come with me," Señor Tiempo told them.

When Maya returned from the lake, Señor Tiempo and the children had disappeared.

"My children! My children!" Maya cried. She ran after them but could not find where Señor Tiempo had taken them.

Maya realized she had been deceived.

Maya was broken-hearted. All her beautiful children were gone.

"Maybe if I gather the pieces of the clay bowls from the lake, my children will return," she said.

She ran to the lake to see if she could find the broken pieces, but the clay had dissolved into the muddy waters.

Maya ran along the edge of the lake, crying into the storm, "*¡Mis niños! ¡Mis niños!*" she wailed. "My children!" Her shrill cry echoed across the lake and sent shivers through all who heard it.

Maya could do nothing but search for her children. She wept and pulled her hair. Her dress grew tattered and her hair matted.

The people of her village heard Maya's cries, but they did not come to help. They were afraid the wailing woman would try to take their own boys and girls. Fearful mothers called their children inside and shut the doors tight.

From that time on the villagers would hear Maya crying as she searched for her children along the edge of the lake. She became known as La Llorona, the woman who wails for her lost children.

Today, Maya may still be heard, weeping for her children along the banks of rivers and lakes.